# As My
# DADDY
# DOES

ISBN 978-1-63630-799-2 (Paperback)
ISBN 978-1-63630-800-5 (Digital)

Covenant Books, Inc.
11661 Hwy 707
Murrells Inlet, SC 29576
www.covenantbooks.com

# As My DADDY DOES

Hannah Fallon

I wake up with the sun and get dressed all by myself, just as my daddy does.

I'm really busy, so I tell my mom, "I've got to go to work," just as my daddy does.

1

I slip on my socks and put on my boots, just as my daddy does.

4

I give my mom a kiss and say, "I'll be back soon," just as my daddy does.

I take my jeep to the garage and give it some gas, just as my daddy does.

I work on my jeep by checking the engine and changing the tires, just as my daddy does.

I step back and put my hands on my hips as I check on the work I've done, just as my daddy does.

11

I've worked hard, and now I sit down and drink a juice box, just as my daddy does.

When I'm done with all the work, I like to have fun,
just as my daddy does.

I take a ride on my four-wheeler and go really fast,
just as my daddy does.

13

I play with my dog by throwing a big stick for her to fetch, just as my daddy does.

Mommy calls out, "Dinner's ready!" I come inside and wash my hands, just as my daddy does.

I eat all my food and thank my mom for my meal, just as my daddy does.

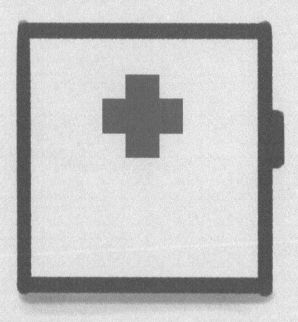

I take a bath to wash the dirt away and brush my teeth before bed, just as my daddy does.

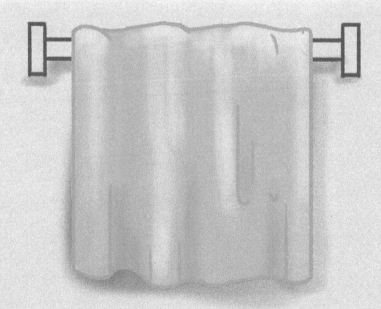

I give my family hugs and kisses and say "I love you" and "good night," just as my daddy does.

I thank God for my blessings and pray for my family and friends, just as my daddy does.

As I drift off to sleep, I smile, knowing I'm just like my daddy.

# About the Author

Hannah Fallon is a wife and mother. She stays at home to care for her two rambunctious boys ages two and four and her precious newborn daughter. She lives on a beautiful piece of land in Ohio and is enjoying raising her kids with all the perks of country living.

CPSIA information can be obtained
at www.ICGtesting.com
Printed in the USA
BVHW021630260421
605873BV00016B/2018

9 781636 307992